Little Penguin's Tale

To Rubin Pfeffer

Copyright © 1989 by Audrey Wood.
All rights reserved. Published by Scholastic Inc.,
555 Broadway, New York, NY 10012,
by arrangement with Harcourt Brace Jovanovich, Inc.

12 11 10 9 8 7 6 5 4 3 2 1   4 5 6 7 8/9

Printed in the U.S.A.   14

First Scholastic printing, December 1993

Little Penguin's Tale

AUDREY WOOD

SCHOLASTIC INC.

New York   Toronto   London   Auckland   Sydney

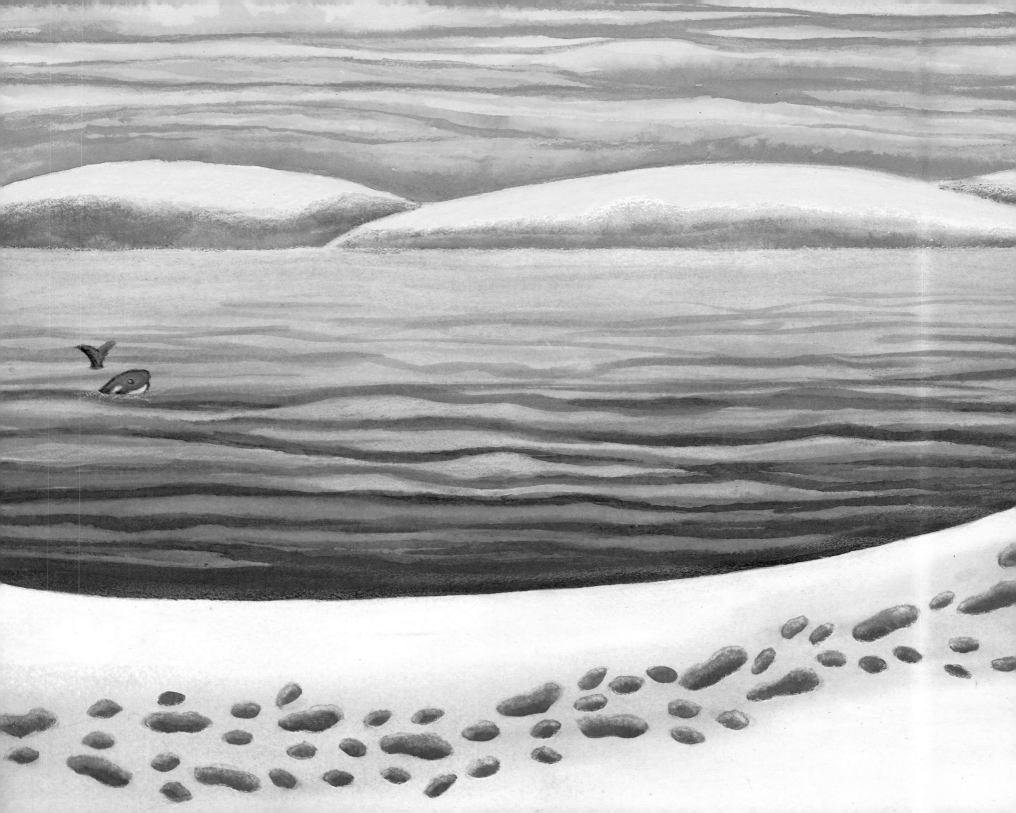

Shhh, little penguins. Now don't make a peep, and Grand Nanny Penguin will tell you a tale of long, long ago.

Once there lived a little penguin just like you. Just like you, except Little Penguin didn't listen to his Grand Nanny's tales.

One morning, at the break of dawn, he snuck off by himself to find some fun in the snowy, polar world.

Up one hill and down another, he soon left all his friends behind.
"Look at me!" Little Penguin cried. "I'm sliding on my tummy
far, far away from home!"

Now everyone knows a little penguin can get lost far, far away from home.

But he didn't.

Right away, Little Penguin came upon a band of dancing gooney birds. They were beating on tin cans and blowing tunes through empty glass bottles.

Little Penguin had never heard such music. It tickled his beak and made him laugh. His feet began to move.

"Look at me!" Little Penguin cried. "I'm dancing with the gooney birds!"

Now everyone knows a little penguin can get into big trouble dancing with the gooney birds.

But he didn't.

Soon they all danced into a rickety boat and sailed out to the Walrus Polar Club.

"Jolly good, old chaps!" a walrus called. "Do come in and have some fun, won't you?"

"Hey, ho!" the gooney birds cheered. "We will."
"Me, too!" Little Penguin said, and he followed them inside.

Little Penguin had never seen such a place. It was a madcap club where animals gathered from all over the world to do whatever they pleased.

Before long, he jumped in the middle and joined the fun.

"Look at me!" Little Penguin cried. "I'm the wildest of them all!"

Now everyone knows a little penguin can get hurt when he's the wildest of them all.

But he didn't.

On and on they danced and played until even the wildest grew weary. Little Penguin could hardly keep his eyes open. So he wandered outside and lay down to take a nap.

"Look at me!" Little Penguin yawned.
"I'm falling asleep by the deep, dark sea."

Now everyone knows a little penguin can get eaten by a whale if he falls asleep by the deep, dark sea.

And that's just what happened.

A great whale opened its mouth and gobbled him up in one bite.

Poor Little Penguin. That was the end of him.

Oh, dear! My goodness! Don't cry, little penguins. It's just a
tale of long ago. And…I suppose it could have ended differently.

Now where was I? Ahhh, yes. Little Penguin fell asleep by the deep, dark sea. Then a great whale opened its mouth and tried to gobble him up.

But Little Penguin was too clever. Quick as a wink, he jumped out
of the whale's mouth, into the rickety boat...

and sailed all the way back home to his Grand Nanny and friends.
But not, mind you, before the great whale managed to nip off a few
of his very best tail feathers.

And that is the end of Little Penguin's tale.